镜子书 · 新编经典童话绘本系列

担当篇

THE STORIES OF MANKIND

人类的故事

[意] 曼纽拉·阿德雷亚尼 绘　　[意] 费德丽卡·玛格林 编　　李静滢 译

SPM 南方传媒　广东人民出版社

· 广州 ·

绘者 **曼纽拉·阿德雷亚尼**

意大利插画师、平面设计师。先后从事平面设计、动画创作、插画绘制工作。

曾获欧洲设计学院（都灵分院）动画专业博士生奖学金。在Làstrego & Testa工作室工作期间，设计制作了《阿拉丁历险记》等一系列动画片，并在意大利国家电视台播放。

2011年起，与基准出版社、学乐印度公司合作，开始了自由插画家的职业生涯。先后创作了《木偶奇遇记》《爱丽丝漫游奇境》《绿野仙踪》《白雪公主》《小王子》和《美女与野兽》等绘本。其绘本作品曾获世界三大绘本大奖之一的"凯特·格林纳威奖"提名。

做个有担当的孩子

　　责任无时无刻不伴随着我们。在生活中，我们充当各种各样的角色，因而也承担着不同的责任。在家里，我们是孩子，要承担孝敬父母的责任；在学校，我们是学生，要承担好好学习的责任；等到长成大人，我们还要承担作为社会的一份子的责任。

　　其实，人类的历史，也是承担责任的过程。西方神话传说中，挪亚担当起拯救人类的责任，在洪水中，将家人和动物带上方舟，才保留了人类文明的火种……

目录

创　世　　　　　　　　　　　　　　　　8

亚当和夏娃　　　　　　　　　　　　　14

挪亚方舟　　　　　　　　　　　　　　20

巴别塔　　　　　　　　　　　　　　　26

约瑟和他的兄弟们　　　　　　　　　　30

力士参孙　　　　　　　　　　　　　　38

大卫与歌利亚　　　　　　　　　　　　44

所罗门　　　　　　　　　　　　　　　48

约　拿　　　　　　　　　　　　　　　54

狮穴中的但以理　　　　　　　　　　　59

创 世

　　最初世界上没有天，也没有地，只有混沌。到处一片荒凉，不适合生存，也不存在生命。我们今天习以为常的伟大非凡的事物，包括山川、大海、平原、森林，那时全都不存在。在黑暗和荒芜中没有任何生命，就连最微小的生物也没有。

　　出于博大无边的爱，上帝开始创造世界。他希望这个世界是完美的。他用了七天的时间来完成这一工作。他做的第一件事是将水分成上下两部分，由此产生了原始的海洋，但是里面既没有鱼也没有藻类。世界仍然漆黑一片，空虚混沌，任何形式的生命都无法生存，哪怕是最低等的生物。

　　出于这个原因，上帝决定，要有光——温暖、强大的光，能让未来的居住者得以在这个世界上繁衍生息，无须再畏惧无边的黑暗。黑暗只会停留在夜晚，夜晚被安排为休息的时间，夜晚的黑暗既可纪念没有光明的可怕往昔，也可反衬出新的光明和希望。

　　第一天过去了，上帝将天与地分离，并将他创造出的苍穹命名为天空。他将天空置于高处，让人可以在下方仰望天空，赞美天空，产生天马行空的幻想。

第二天结束了，上帝还在继续他的工作，他把水汇聚在一起，形成大洋、大海、湖泊、河流、小溪和沼泽。露出来的干燥陆地有时会被雨水滋润，上帝让陆地长出了各种各样的植物，并分隔出了大片的平原和森林，树木可以提供木材和阴凉处。他又让某些种类的植物结出果实和种子，让它们长得郁郁葱葱。

此时的世界已经比以前舒适美好了，为发展更复杂的生命形式提供了理想的环境。

第四天，上帝为他已经创造出的事物添加了两盏巨大的"灯"。一盏灯是又大又明亮的太阳，能在白天提供光明和温暖。另一盏灯是体积较小、亮度较暗的月亮，能够照亮夜晚。

现在，上帝创造的世界可以成为生物的家园了。

第五天，上帝让江河湖海遍布各种鱼类和其他水生动物，例如水母、海豚和鲸；又创造了天空中形形色色的飞鸟，既有蜂鸟这样的小鸟，也有鹈鹕这样的大鸟，同时也创造出了其他长着翅膀能够飞行的动物。

　　地球上变得生机盎然。水里游弋着各种各样外形奇异、色彩绚丽的水生动物，它们用鳃呼吸，用鳍迅速划水。蓝天上飞翔着成群的鸟，它们鸣啭啼唱，有的拍打着翅膀从一个地方飞到另一个地方，有的展开双翼乘风翱翔。上帝觉得这些生物都很美好，于是要求水生动物和有翼动物多多繁衍，遍布世界的各个角落，哪怕是最遥不可及的地方。

　　上帝出色的创造值得叹服，但上帝还不满意。他感到缺少了重要的东西，因此，在第六天，他又让大地上出现了各种动物，例如山羊、牛和绵羊等可以驯服的牲畜，狮子、大象和熊等难以接近的野兽，小蜥蜴和大蛇等爬行动物。

这六天里，上帝创造出的万物都妙不可言，值得赞美，但上帝仍然感到缺失了某些东西，他尽了全力，要让世界在他完工时十全十美。于是他按自身的形象创造出了另外一种动物，那就是人。上帝创造了男人和女人，他们彼此不同，但是同等重要，他们结合在一起时，就可以生儿育女，在大地上生生不息。

上帝交给人一项重要的工作，那就是照顾动物和植物，带着爱心养育它们。人可以从土地上得到生存繁衍所需的一切，上帝将各种蔬菜和种子赐予人们作为食物，将青草赐予牛羊作为饲料，让人们衣食无忧。

第六天结束时，上帝看着他创造出的一切，感到非常高兴。上面是天空，下面是大地。天空中的太阳、月亮和星辰照亮了世界，指引着道路。大地被水域、森林、平原和沙漠覆盖，动物和人类可以在大地上和平地生活。眼前的一切，标志着上帝已经完美地实现了自己的计划，也体现出了他对所创造的世界的无限热爱。

在第七天，上帝完成了全部工作，于是决定休息一下，自己悠闲地欣赏起他在天空中和大地上创造出来的一切。这一整天他什么也没有做，只是观赏着眼前奇异的景象，观赏着生机勃勃的大树、争芳斗艳的花朵、形形色色的动物和人。上帝决定，从此以后就把第七天定为休息日，在这一天休息并礼赞这独一无二的地球。

在西方故事中，我们周围的一切事物——天地、日月、所有生灵——就是这样创造出来的。

亚当和夏娃

　　世界上第一个人的故事要追溯到远古时代，那时世界才刚刚被创造出来。上帝从地面取一捧尘土，按自己的形象造出了男人，名叫亚当。但是刚创造出来的人没有生命，就像个木偶。上帝将生命的气息吹入他的鼻孔，他才开始呼吸走动，成了有灵的活人。上帝为男人建造了一座伊甸园，作为他的家园。伊甸园位于东方，里面生长着各种植物，结着永远吃不完的水果。园中还有一棵独特的生命之树，如果吃了这棵树的果实，就能分辨善与恶。上帝向男人展示伊甸园中的各种奇观时，和他讲得非常清楚：这棵生命树的果实是禁止食用的。

　　就这样，世界上的第一个人开始在这个迷人的地方生活，以园中生长的植物和水果为食，无须劳苦，无忧无虑。

　　很快，这个人就开始感到孤独，所以上帝决定让各种各样的动物陪伴他。

　　上帝把天空中飞的、地上跑的、水里游的各种动物一个个带到男人面前，叫他给它们起名字。他给各种动物逐一起了名字。但是，尽管身边有各种各样的动物，他仍然觉得自己还没找到想要的伴侣。

　　上帝意识到，男人需要的是与自己相似的生灵，能够在一起交谈，能够共度时光。于是，上帝让男人陷入沉睡，然后取出他的一根肋骨，造出了女人。

　　男人醒来后惊叹女人的美丽，这新的生命是他身体的一部分，因此也是他生命的一部分。上帝命令他们从那一刻起成为夫妻，他们的结合将长久存在，直至永远。这对夫妻在伊甸园里幸福地生活了一段时间，他们赤身裸体，却并不以此为耻，也没有任何忧虑困扰。

女人有一天遇到了一条大蛇。大蛇问她："听说你们人类不能吃生命树上的果实，这是真的吗？"

女人回答说："园里的所有果子我们都可以吃，除了园子正中央那棵树上的果实，因为我们吃了就会死。"

蛇回答说这不是真的，他们绝不会因为吃一口果子就死亡。"实际上，"蛇又引诱说，"吃了那果子之后，你就会像上帝一样，知晓一切。"

女人走到那棵树下仔细观察，第一次注意到生命之树上的果实比其他果实都更诱人。她久久思考着蛇说的话，最终无法抗拒诱惑。她摘了一个果子，拿给丈夫。

他们一起吃下了这颗果实，接着就立刻意识到自己赤裸着身体。这果子让他们知道了以前不知道的善与恶，因此他们找了些无花果树叶缝在一起，遮挡自己的身体。

晚些时候，男人听到上帝走来的声音，连忙跑开躲在一棵树后面。

"你们为什么要跑开？"上帝看见男人想躲藏，就问道。

“因为我赤身裸体，不好意思见你。”

“你怎么知道你是赤身裸体的？”上帝吃了一惊，接着又问道，“难道你吃了生命之树的果实？”

男人点了点头，上帝问他为什么要这样做。

“我妻子给我吃的，我没能抵挡住品尝它的诱惑。”

上帝转身问女人：“我和你们说过这种果子不能吃，你为什么还要吃？”

女人就讲了自己遇见蛇的事情，说蛇欺骗了她，告诉她吃了这棵树的果实后不会有什么严重的后果。

上帝发了怒，首先诅咒蛇说：“因为你所做的事，你和你的后代终生都将在地面上爬行吃尘土。

“你和女人之间，没有友谊，只有仇恨。

“你想咬伤她的脚，她想踩烂你的头。”

接着，上帝的怒火又转向了男人和女人。上帝向他们宣布，他们现在必须辛苦劳作，才能从地里得到他们以前毫不费力就能采摘的食物。

上帝把男人和女人逐出了神奇的伊甸园，罚他们永远在贫瘠的土地上生活。

男人和女人被迫离开他们的乐土时，亚当给妻子起名叫夏娃，从此夏娃将成为世人的母亲。

亚当和夏娃结合以后，生下了两个相貌性格迥异的孩子，一个是该隐，一个是亚伯。该隐喜欢种地，亚伯喜欢牧羊。

该隐和亚伯长大以后，有一天决定要把每天的一部分收获奉献给上帝。该隐献上了他收获的最鲜美的果实，亚伯献上了他的一些绵羊。上帝更钟爱亚伯的献祭，这让该隐怨恨起上帝和亚伯。该隐怒火中烧，加害了亚伯。

上帝知道了该隐的所作所为，罚他离开家园，不得过宁静的生活，即使比以前加倍辛苦地劳作，也未必能得到最微薄的收获。

该隐接受了自己的命运，去往伊甸园东边的挪得之地。他在那里娶妻生子，给孩子起名以诺。以诺在该地建了一座城，称为以诺城，他成了一个大家族的首领。

亚当和夏娃的这两个儿子，一个为兄所害，另一个被放逐，让他们非常痛苦。后来亚当和夏娃又生了一个孩子，名叫塞特。塞特给这对夫妇的生活带来了新的欢乐。

挪亚方舟

这是个美妙的世界，很多年里，人和动物一起过着和平宁静的生活。清澈的河水泛着银光，色彩斑斓的鱼在河里游来游去，留下一串串气泡。冷冽的湖泊深处是各种生物的家园。波涛起伏的海面下隐匿着大小不一、形态奇异的动物。森林茂密，群山巍峨，漫山遍野生长着各种树木果蔬，峰顶的白雪终年不化。成群的食草动物聚集在绿意葱茏的草原上，伺机捕猎的食肉动物尾随着它们。鸟儿在天空中展翅飞翔，一些动物甚至适应了沙漠这样的环境。谁都不缺食物，世界是如此和谐美好。

然而，愉快的岁月逐渐成了过去，人们开始进入悲惨的时代。

男男女女都变得贪婪、傲慢，他们忘记了大自然的美好，忘记了他们应该为此感谢上帝。战争、腐败和仇恨取代了和平、正义和仁爱。其他动物也失去了安宁的生活。世界重新陷入了混乱无序的状态。

上帝观察着，等待着，希望人类能够悔改，重新遵循上帝的规则，但他最终意识到，他所创造的世界再也无法重归昔日的辉煌。他痛心疾首，决定重头再来，就像一个画家放弃修改一幅画，伸手去取一块空白的新画布一样。要做到这一点，唯一的办法就是让洪水席卷一切邪恶，只有正义的、美好的人和物才能留存下来，再度兴盛繁荣。

上帝选择了挪亚。挪亚和别人不一样，他一直听上帝的话，关心家人，认真照料饲养的动物，每天都赞美上帝。

上帝对挪亚说："我怀着沉重的心情做出了这个决定，我要发起暴风雨，用大洪水淹没整个世界，消灭一切邪恶之物。我不想让你和你的家人陷入危险，并且，我希望能以你为新人类的开端，让人类变得更加友善，更加公平。因此，我命令你造一艘

方舟，一艘巨大的船，要能容纳七对干净的畜类和一对不干净的畜类，要用结实的木材造船，内外涂上松脂防水。你还必须加盖一个船顶，好挡住雨水。时候一到我会通知你，你要把动物、家人和足够的食物带进方舟。"

听了上帝所说的话，挪亚十分震惊，但还是按照上帝的吩咐开始准备。他锯好了一块块结实的木板，将它们连接在一起，把整艘船建好后又在里里外外涂好了松脂，储备好了食物。

上帝再次向挪亚宣布，洪水很快就要暴发了。"七天后将连降暴雨四十天四十夜。你要在这一天到来之前按我所说做好一切准备，这样你就会平安无事。"

当时六百岁的挪亚完全听从上帝的指示，把各种动物赶进方舟，然后叫他的妻子、三个儿子和三个儿媳登船避难。三个儿子的名字是闪、含和雅弗。

第七天到了，天空乌云密布，方舟外面漆黑如夜。

太阳不见了踪影，黑暗笼罩着大地。几秒钟后，滂沱大雨倾泻而下，冰冷的雨水冲击着树木和房屋。大水淹没了平原，淹没了森林。海水不停上涨，巨浪冲垮了堤岸，

淹没了沙漠，淹没了高山。大雨下个不停，洪水持续泛滥，淹没了整个大地，就连最高的山顶也消失在汹涌浩大的水面之下。

方舟浮在水面上，随着水势漂流。挪亚从船顶的小窗户向外眺望，除了肆虐的暴雨什么也看不到。

大雨不停地下了四十天四十夜。方舟中的挪亚一家人和各种动物都安然无恙，他们吃着准备好的食物，满怀希望等待着暴雨停歇。

一阵强劲的风突然吹起，吹散了乌云，吹遍了大地，一些地方的水渐渐退去。到了洪水后的第七个月，挪亚的方舟搁浅在亚拉腊山。又过了三个月，群峰开始露出水面。

整个世界似乎仍然淹没在水下，因此挪亚放出一只乌鸦，又放出了一只鸽子，让它们去看看大水退了没有。它们没有找到可以落脚的地面，都飞了回来。

洪水太大了，过了好些天仍然遍地都是水。终于有一天，当挪亚再次将鸽子放出去探寻外界情况时，它的嘴里衔着橄榄枝飞了回来。挪亚欣喜若狂，因为他知道大地终于又焕发出了生机。上帝信守了对挪亚的承诺，他们安全了！

"挪亚，"上帝呼唤他说，"你和你的家人可以离开方舟了，世界已经恢复了往日的样子，从现在开始直至未来的世世代代，这里都将是你的家园，也将是你带上船的所有动物的家园。你得到了我的祝福，我和你约定，再也不会有这样毁灭一切的大洪水。作为立约的凭证，天空中将出现色彩斑斓的彩虹，来纪念天空与大地之间的誓约。"上帝刚说完，天空中就出现了一道壮观的彩虹。

上帝继续说："所有见到彩虹的人都将记起我们立的誓约，也将记起，上帝爱护所有善良正直的人。"

挪亚当起了农夫，开心地照料葡萄园。有时他会抬头仰望天空，寻找彩虹。彩虹会让他想起上帝对他的承诺，对他的后代的承诺，对他所缔造的新世界的承诺。

巴别塔

起初，人类是不分民族的，领土也并没有边界。所有的人都讲同一种语言，人人都能理解别人所讲的语言，因此彼此交流毫无困难。居住在北部的人与居住在南部的人是平等的，在东部定居的人与在西部定居的人也没什么不同。人们平静地生活在一起，定期举行聚会，庆祝上帝赐予人们非凡的世界。

有一天，一些人来到远东的示拿地，在那里建起了一座城，这座城市比其他城市更大、更雄伟。这些人想与自然媲美，想建造出与山脉、森林和海洋一样壮观的东西。

这是人们第一次尝试修建如此气势恢宏的建筑，为此人们用大型砖窑烧制了很多砖。这些砖比通常使用的石材坚固得多，与松香黏合后比普通砂浆更加耐用。

人们决定要在示拿地城的中央建一座能够通天的高塔，其规模之巨大，将让所有的人都为之惊叹。那将是直入云霄的高塔，从下面仰望时无法看到塔顶，因为塔顶隐没在云层中了。

在城市里修建房屋和其他大型建筑需要投入大量的人力物力。匠人和力工在建筑师和工程师的带领下日复一日、年复一年地工作，盖好了很多房子，但建造通天塔的难度要大得多。

通天塔的修建工作稳步推进，建好了一层又一层，人们看在眼里，心中非常自豪。

"这是有史以来人类创造出的最美的东西！"有人这样感慨。

"世界上没有什么能与这座塔相比！"有人这样赞叹。

有人提议说："现在我们建了这座塔，就该给它起个名字，好与世界其他地方区分开来。"

"对呀，"另外的人回答，"我们与其他地方的人都不一样。我们已经建起了这座城市，还有这座宏伟的高塔！"

"对啊，"更多的人附和道，"我们与众不同。我们更优秀，因为我们修起了独一无二、无与伦比的建筑。"

示拿地城的喧嚣声传到了上帝的耳朵里。上帝一直在关注着他所创造的世界。他创造了人类，目的是让人们和谐相处，与其他动物共享这个世界，所有的人都是平等的，没有优劣之分。人们的这些话语让上帝非常伤心。他从尘土中造出人类，并不是让人挑战上帝并试图取代上帝的位置！

上帝对修建通天塔和赞美通天塔的人感到失望，但是上帝也意识到，挑战上帝和超越上帝是人的本性。上帝没有用闪电击毁高塔，也没有派使者劝说人们恢复理性。上帝所做的只是把人们分成不同的国家，让人们具有不同的特征，讲不同的语言，互相无法沟通。

结果，示拿地这座城变得荒芜，城中宏伟的通天塔此后被称为"巴别塔"，意思是"混乱之处"。

的确，正是在修建巴别塔之后，人们才开始讲不同的语言，人们之间的交流才变得极端困难。

约瑟和他的兄弟们

雅各有好几个孩子。身为父亲，他爱每个孩子，不过对最小的孩子约瑟格外宠爱，这与他老年得子有关，当时他以为自己不会再有孩子了。约瑟从出生起就成了父亲心头的宝贝。雅各对约瑟总是非常亲热，送给他很多精心准备的礼物。

约瑟的哥哥们开始妒忌他。后来，约瑟做了些不寻常的梦，梦见自己将有不同寻常的人生，还会接受人们的跪拜，这就更招致哥哥们的嫉恨。

雅各让约瑟的哥哥们去示剑附近放羊，后来不放心，就让约瑟去看看他们是否顺利。少年约瑟想让父亲高兴，就立刻动身找到了正在牧羊的哥哥们。可是，被嫉恨冲昏头脑的哥哥们却把约瑟卖给了前往埃及的商人。

约瑟就这样被卖为奴，被商队带到遥远的埃及。他的哥哥们收了二十元钱，回到家里告诉父亲说，他最爱的小儿子被野兽吃了。

雅各在迦南为儿子的死伤心哭泣时，约瑟被卖到了法老的护卫长波提乏家里。约瑟很快就向主人波提乏证明，交给他做的各种事情他都能做得很好，波提乏提拔约瑟当了管家。糟糕的是，波提乏的妻子注意到了约瑟，喜欢上了他。约瑟敬重波提乏，拒绝了她的求爱，没想到却遭到她的报复。约瑟受到她的诬陷，被关进了监狱。

约瑟不仅是父亲最爱的孩子，他还拥有上帝的爱，上帝一直关注着约瑟。在上帝的安排下，监狱长很快就了解到了约瑟的才华，因此让他负责管理监狱的各种事务。

约瑟在监狱里经常为人解梦。他一直有解梦的能力，这是他与众不同的天赋。

正因为会解梦，约瑟后来见到了法老。法老做了两个噩梦，感到很不安。他觉得这两个噩梦是对他的警示，但他对梦的含义一无所知。

　　法老的司酒长建议法老召见约瑟，因为约瑟曾成功地帮他解梦。法老马上宣约瑟觐见。

　　"我很不安，"法老说，"前几天晚上，我梦见了七头肥壮的牛，然后是七头瘦牛；接着又梦见了七枝饱满的谷穗，我眼看着它们变得干瘪。我知道这一定预示着什么，但我不知道是什么……"

　　约瑟解释说："七头肥牛和七枝饱满的谷穗一样，都预示着大丰收的七年，而七头瘦牛和七枝干瘪的谷穗，预示着七个荒年。在丰收的年头必须贮备起足够的粮食，这样在大地干旱、颗粒无收时，人们就不会挨饿了。"

　　听了约瑟的话，法老很伤脑筋。如果约瑟的预言是正确的，法老就必须认真对待，否则发生旱灾后他的王国可能会为饥荒所困。虽然心存困惑，法老还是相信了约瑟的解释，并决定任命约瑟为宰相。法老亲手给约瑟戴上戒指，表明他同意约瑟的决策。

约瑟从奴隶和囚徒一下就变成了地位显赫的官员，法老派他管理全国的物资，确保物资充足、国家繁荣。正如他所预言的那样，埃及连续七年降雨充沛，粮食高产，收获的麦子超出人们预料。约瑟亲自督查，下令将所有余粮都贮存在仓库里。七个丰年之后，埃及果然发生了旱灾，植物都枯萎了，约瑟及时下令打开粮仓，把粮食供给人们和动物食用。

旱灾不仅影响了尼罗河流域，还蔓延到了邻近地区。雅各所在的迦南也发生了饥荒。雅各听说埃及有粮食，就派他的儿子们带着钱去埃及买粮。

约瑟的哥哥们来到埃及，正巧遇到了在国内巡视的约瑟。

可以想象，哥哥们没有认出约瑟，他们只知道眼前这人是个大人物，就向他鞠躬叩拜。约瑟却一眼就认出了他们，也想起了他们对他的所作所为，因此约瑟说他们是奸细，想让警卫把他们赶走。但他三思之后又改变了主意。他听说，自己离开家之后，母亲又生了个弟弟，这让他内心激动，非常想见见这个弟弟。他又和哥哥们说，他可以给他们麦子，但是他们必须把小弟弟带过来见他。

约瑟的哥哥们仍然没有认出约瑟。约瑟派人给他们的袋子装满了麦子，他们还以为那人就只是埃及的宰相。回到家中，兄弟们把遇到的埃及官员提出的要求告诉了父亲雅各。

雅各不同意把小儿子便雅悯送到遥远的埃及，他担心会失去便雅悯，就像当年失去深爱的约瑟一样。

又过了一段时间，雅各家里的粮食眼看就要吃完了。他无计可施，只能妥协。

便雅悯和哥哥们一起出发去埃及，再次拜见宰相。

约瑟热情地款待了他们。尽管他的哥哥们当年对他残忍无情，他还是想原谅他们。

约瑟派车接他的兄弟们与他和家人一起用餐，这让他的兄弟们非常惊讶。他们依然不知道约瑟还活着，而且就站在他们面前。约瑟吩咐人给他们麦子，允许他们离开，他们惊惧交加，总有一种不祥的感觉。

几兄弟在回家的路上被一些埃及士兵拦住了，要检查他们的粮食袋子，并且在便雅悯的袋子里发现了一只银杯。那银杯其实是约瑟指示他的手下藏在那里的，因为约瑟想最后考验一下他的兄弟们。他们被带回到宫殿，约瑟要考验他们是否爱便雅悯，就说便雅悯偷走了杯子，必须留下为奴。他的哥哥们上前恳求约瑟让便雅悯回家，说他们担心父亲，不忍心就这样回去告诉可怜的父亲他又失去了一个儿子。约瑟不禁为之动容，于是告知他们自己的身份，请他们回迦南去把父亲和家人都带到埃及。

雅各最初不愿离开祖先留下的土地，但最终还是决定到埃及去。

雅各之所以同意去埃及，是因为他知道，到了埃及就能再次拥抱他一直认为早已不在人世的儿子。

雅各在所有儿子的陪伴下愉快地度过了自己生命的最后几年，临终时非常平静。

约瑟的兄弟们担心约瑟会在父亲去世后报复他们。他们不知道，约瑟已经发自内心、诚心诚意地原谅了他们，并不是为了取悦父亲才装出来的。

"不要担心，"约瑟的兄弟们聚在宫殿里时，约瑟向他们做出了保证，"我不想伤害你们。这就是上帝的意旨，上帝希望事情这样发展，希望我们是今天这样，我们一家人才在这里团聚，不用担心饥荒或更严重的危险。"

约瑟有一颗宽容仁爱的心，能够善待曾经伤害过他的人，他自己也得到了长寿和幸福生活的回报。他亲眼看着自己的孩子们长大成人，看着孙子们来到世界，一直活了一百一十岁，才在家中安详地去世。

力士参孙

　　每个人都是独一无二的，但是有些人从小就并非凡人，他们被选中来完成伟大的壮举，他们的出生就是奇迹。参孙的命运就是这样，他注定要成为英雄，成为他的同胞的救星。

　　那时，以色列人处于非利士人的统治下，遭到非利士人的蔑视，无法按照自己的意愿生活。很多以色列人都希望有人来帮他们重获自由。

　　在非利士人管辖的一座城市里，住着一个善良而又虔诚的以色列人，名叫玛挪亚，他妻子和他一样既善良又虔诚。让他们感到遗憾的是，两个人一直没有孩子。有一天，一个天使前来指示玛挪亚的妻子，说她很快将成为母亲，这让她十分惊讶。天使又告诉她，从孕育的那一天起，这个孩子就注定要奉献一生，他在生活中将恪守一些规则，包括永远不吃不洁的食物，不剃发。玛挪亚的妻子就更加吃惊了。

　　她担心自己未能完全理解神的使者的话，于是叫来丈夫玛挪亚。天使又把需要恪守的戒律给玛挪亚讲了一遍。

　　在玛挪亚和妻子的希冀中，参孙出生了。他渐渐长大，越来越有力量，越来越勇敢，也越来越出名。见到他的人有的害怕他，有的敬重他。但是参孙的性格也有弱点，这弱点让他看不见将要发生的危险，结果会让他陷入困境。

　　参孙在亭拿深深爱上了一个非利士女孩，决意要娶她，尽管他的父母担心他以后会与女孩的家人发生冲突，并不赞成这桩婚事。

　　参孙父母的担心是有道理的。参孙与非利士人无法融洽相处，最后发生了武力冲突。非利士人要抓参孙，以色列人中的犹大居民害怕非利士人报复，率先去找参孙，把参孙绑了起来交给非利士人。参孙到达非利士人的驻地后，肌肉发力，紧紧绑在身上的绳子全都断了，好像火烧过的麻一样落到他的脚上。参孙进行反击，顺手抓起身边一头死驴的颌骨，像铁锤一样抡了起来，很快就击溃了一千人组成的军队。

参孙打败了非利士人，觉得口渴，于是呼告上帝。泉水立刻就从他脚下涌了出来。

后来参孙搬到迦萨，在梭烈谷又遇到了一个漂亮女子。他爱上了这个名叫大利拉的女子，却不知道大利拉对他有所隐瞒——非利士人的首领要她设法探听出参孙的一切秘密。

大利拉很聪明，想方设法诱哄参孙说出自己的秘密。只要她能找到参孙力大无穷的奥秘，非利士人就能彻底击败他了。

参孙在很长一段时间里都没对大利拉说实话。他先后几次骗大利拉说，要想打败他，可以拿七根没干的青绳子把他捆住，或者拿没用过的新绳子把他捆住，或者把他的头发拴在门上。大利拉每次都会把参孙的话告诉非利士人。非利士人试了这几种方法，但都失败了。

然而，参孙太爱大利拉了，终于有一天，他没再欺骗大利拉。

"你一定要知道，"他说，"我的力量就来自我从未剪过的头发。如果有人剪掉了我的头发，我就会失去神力，和常人一样了。"

到了晚上，大利拉哄参孙睡在她腿上，等参孙睡着后剪掉了他的头发。

一直等在外面的非利士人冲进房间，刺瞎了参孙的眼睛，把他带到迦萨，用链子锁住，逼他在监牢里推磨。

参孙饱受羞辱和嘲笑，活在深深的绝望中，但是他的头发又慢慢地长起来了。

非利士统治者决定向他们的神灵大衮献祭。数千人聚集在神殿里，还把参孙从狱中带到神殿里戏弄取乐。

参孙利用这个机会执行了上帝的计划。他靠在神殿的柱子上，呼喊道："上帝啊，求求你，让我重获出生时得到的力量，让我和非利士人同归于尽吧！"说完参孙用力推倒了支撑神殿的柱子，整座建筑轰然倒塌，压在众人身上。参孙就这样告别了尘世。

参孙是个英雄，他曾在爱的骗局中迷失方向，但最终重新获得了失去的力量和勇气，勇敢地接受了命运。

大卫与歌利亚

想象一下吧，一个比你高不了多少的少年迎接巨人的挑战，会是什么样的情形呢？是不是有些不可思议呢？大卫在成为以色列王之前，就曾有过这样的英勇行为。我们来讲一下他的故事吧。

当时，非利士人聚集起来，在以弗大悯扎营，要向以色列人开战，以色列人在附近扎营，准备迎战非利士人的军队。

非利士人的队伍里有一个来自迦特的人，名叫歌利亚，身材彪悍，气势汹汹，战无不胜。他每天都走出军营，挥舞着武器向以色列人叫喊，问他们谁敢出来应战。

他挥舞着沉重的铁枪，就像挥动树枝一样轻松。他的一身铠甲在阳光下熠熠生辉。

歌利亚声如洪钟，以色列人只是听到他的声音就已经心惊胆战，竟然没有一人敢站出来应战。双方陷入了僵持状态。

大卫那时还只是个少年，平常跟着父亲牧羊。有一天，这个红头发的小伙子按父亲的吩咐来到军营探望几个哥哥，准备把他们的军饷给父亲带回去。他听到歌利亚出来叫阵，却并不害怕，反而十分好奇，四下询问这是怎么回事。

当时的以色列王是扫罗，扫罗听说了少年大卫与众不同的表现，就派人把大卫找来，想让他解释一下。

还没等扫罗开口问他，大卫就说："我要去和他战斗。"扫罗吃惊地说："你还是个孩子，他那么强壮，而且身经百战，你凭什么觉得自己能与他抗衡？"

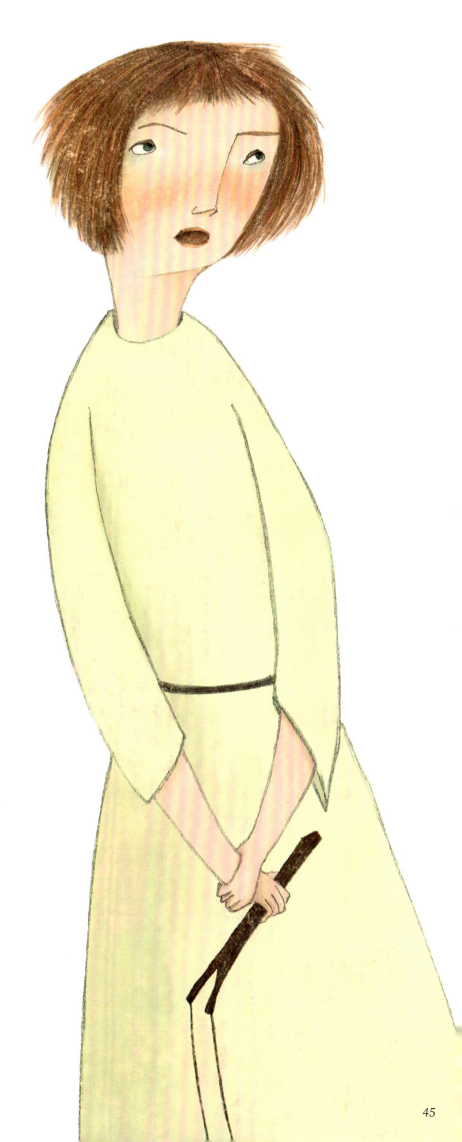

大卫回答说：“我为父亲放羊时，遇到过狮子，遇到过熊，遇到过各种各样的野兽，我总能战胜它们。”

扫罗帮大卫穿上盔甲，但是大卫不习惯这样穿戴，于是又脱下盔甲，从溪涧中捡了五块石子，拿着投石弓，就去应战了。

歌利亚看到大卫走上前来，不禁发出一阵大笑。笑够了之后，他恐吓大卫说要把他撕成碎片，拿他的尸体去喂野兽。

大卫回答说，他会杀死歌利亚，而歌利亚的死将意味着非利士人的惨败。说完，大卫勇敢无畏地冲向身高力壮的歌利亚，从口袋里掏出石子，用投石弓向歌利亚射了出去。石子正中歌利亚的前额，把他打倒在地。大卫跑上前，把歌利亚的刀从刀鞘中拔出来，砍下了歌利亚的头。

非利士人看到他们的勇士死了，立刻纷纷逃跑。以色列军队在后面追击他们。

大卫的事迹很快流传开来，人们都为他欢呼，对他赞不绝口。一个少年竟能有勇有谋，杀死敌方最强悍的武士。

他依靠一把投石弓和无尽的勇气，就战胜了力量巨大的敌人。

所罗门

英雄通常都是勇敢、强大的人，在极少数情况下，也被赋予大智慧，这是上帝赐予的礼物。

所罗门就是这样一个幸运的人，他出类拔萃，才智超群。所罗门自己向上帝求取这件礼物。当他登基为王之后，本可以向上帝求取财富、永生、俊美、力量，求取一个有权势的人希望得到的一切，但他却请求上帝赐予他智慧，让他可以永远受理性的指引，可以治理好父亲大卫留给他的国家。

所罗门的智慧成了众人皆知的美谈，很多人从遥远的地方慕名来到他的宫殿，请他明辨是非。

有一天，两个女人带着一个婴儿来见所罗门，两人都自称是这个孩子的母亲。"这个女人和我住同一间房，"一个女人先开口说，"我们都生下了一个男孩。一天晚上，我带着孩子一起睡觉，孩子就在我身边，但是第二天早上

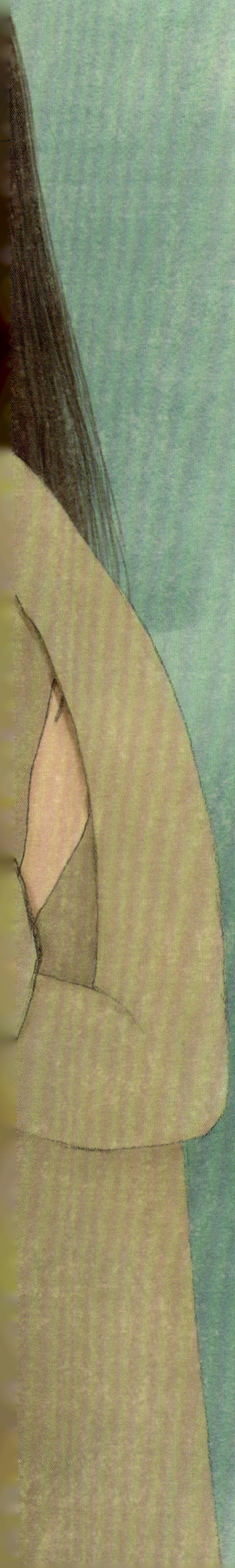

醒来时，孩子就死了。我仔细一看，发现死去的婴
儿不是我的儿子，而是她的儿子。她是在自己的孩
子死去后偷偷换走了我的儿子。"

"这不是真的！"轮到另一个女人讲话时，她
反对说，"我怀中的婴儿就是我生下来的孩子，我
从他出生那一刻起就一直照料他。这个女人失去了
她自己的孩子，就想用我的孩子代替他，但我绝对
不能让她得逞！"

听了两个人的不同说法后，所罗门想了一想，然后离开房间。过了片刻，他走了回来，手里拿着一把锋利的长刀。

"我不知道这婴儿究竟是谁的孩子，你们两人争执不下，所以我现在就将孩子劈成两半，你们各得一半。"所罗门说话的态度非常强硬，让人无话可说。

"不，不要这样做！"第一个女人痛苦地嚷了起来，"千万不要杀死我儿子，我宁可把儿子让给她。"

另一个女人则说："那就这样吧！这样我们就不用再争了。"

所罗门笑了。现在他知道谁才是孩子真正的母亲了。

"只有真正的母亲才会愿意为她的孩子做任何事情，为了让孩子免于伤害，她甚至可以放弃养育他的机会。同意杀死孩子的女人撒了谎，不值得任何人同情。把孩子交给第一个女人吧。"

所罗门公正地判过很多疑案，这只是其中之一。由于他的睿智，他在国内和国外都享有很高的声望。

所罗门的名声也传到了希巴女王的耳朵里，她对此十分好奇，于是带着随从长途跋涉去见所罗门，想知道他是否真的和传说中一样知识渊博。到达所罗门的王宫后，她向所罗门提出了各种错综复杂难以回答的问题，试图抓住他的漏洞，证明他只是个普通人。最后，希巴女王不得不承认，所罗门与众不同，拥有非凡的智慧。她赞美了所罗门的聪明才智。

希巴女王参观了王宫的各个房间，眼前辉煌气派的景象大大出乎她的意料。她早已对华丽的建筑和财富习以为常，但她从来没想过会有人设计建造出如此宏伟的、完美的宫殿。

希巴女王与所罗门告别之前，明确地表达了自己对他的欣赏。她给所罗门留下了一百二十件珍贵的礼物，包括黄金、香料和宝石。

出于对客人的尊重，所罗门接受了这些礼物，但最让他感动的是女王所说的话："祝福您的王国、您周围的人民，您拥有非凡的智慧，在您的领导下，您的国家是多么幸运。"

的确，所罗门比任何人都聪明，他知道"名望重于财富，尊敬重于金银"的道理。

约　拿

先知约拿经历过很多非凡奇特、不可思议的事。他曾经在海上漂泊，曾经和巨大的鱼亲密接触，曾经在异域宣讲布道。

为什么这些事情全都会发生在约拿身上呢？原因就是约拿心里怀疑上帝传递给他的信息，因此上帝要考验他。

有一天，上帝叫约拿去尼尼微城，劝那些邪恶的、不诚实的人悔改。

约拿觉得这项任务太艰难了，是不可能完成的，所以没有去。他朝相反的方向逃跑了，登上了一条开往他施的船。

这艘船刚驶出港口，就在海上遇到了可怕的暴风雨。海上掀起了滔天巨浪，把船打得上下颠簸。狂风猛烈地撕扯着船帆，让船无法向正确的方向航行。

船员们吓坏了，不知道他们能不能在肆虐的风暴中幸免于难。约拿十分清楚，这风暴是上帝安排的，因为上帝要惩罚他不守诺言。约拿怜悯那些惊恐万状的船员，于是告诉他们，只要他们把他扔进海里，任他自生自灭，就能平息上帝的愤怒。

船员们不忍心这样做，但是没有别的办法，只能把约拿扔进大海。顿时，风住了，海面一片平静。

约拿要经受的考验还没有结束。上帝让一条大鱼把约拿吞到了肚子里。约拿在大鱼肚子里过了三天三夜，他向上帝虔诚地祈祷，请求上帝宽恕。最后，上帝让大鱼把约拿吐到了海滩上。

"你现在会按我的要求去尼尼微吗？"上帝又一次问约拿。

约拿二话不说，立刻出发去那罪恶之城，希望能让上帝满意。他一到尼尼微就开

始传扬上帝的话，很快就说服人们改邪归正了。

约拿并没有沾沾自喜，反而觉得生气。他原本以为尼尼微人会对他的话无动于衷，上帝会将这座城市夷为平地。

约拿在尼尼微城外搭了一间小屋，气呼呼地坐在门前。为了让约拿明白他的错误，上帝让这间小屋旁边长出了一棵枝繁叶茂的蓖麻树。约拿非常喜欢这棵树，因为它可以为他遮挡强烈的阳光。但是第二天，一条蠕虫咬了树根，树就枯萎了。

约拿躺在自己的小屋里，被炽烈的阳光晒得痛不欲生。

上帝对约拿说："这棵蓖麻树生长出来后很快就枯萎了，你并没有照料过它，却还是因为它的枯萎闷闷不乐。尼尼微城里有成千上万的人，难道我不该关心这座城市的命运吗？"

约拿这才明白，自己之前未能理解上帝的悲悯之心。尼尼微人虽然做过错事，但是能诚心悔过，因此他们应该得到宽恕。

狮穴中的但以理

　　玛代人大利乌统治波斯时，王国里有一个正直而虔诚的人，名叫但以理。他忠于国王，同时也恪守上帝的律令。大利乌王对但以理委以重任，要让他管理全国事务，可以和国王一样做出重要的决策，这样的任命在王室引起了轰动。其他官员得不到这么大的权力，因此都十分嫉妒但以理，设法要找出他的错误，抓住他的把柄，却都没有成功。但以理并不理会他们的挑衅。

　　官员们发现但以理忠心处理国事，无可挑剔，于是决定设下陷阱。他们私下里去见大利乌王，请他重立一项古时曾有过的禁令，禁止人们在三十天内向国王以外的人或神明祷告，违令者将被处死。大利乌王不明白他们为什么提出这样的要求，他们就解释说，这对玛代人和波斯人重获昔日的辉煌至关重要。

　　大利乌王最终签署了该禁令，他并不知道官员们是想陷害但以理。但以理仍与往常一样，每天三次打开朝向圣地耶路撒冷方向的窗户，在窗前跪下向上帝祷告。

　　但以理听说了这项禁令，但他觉得自己并没有做错什么，他向上帝祷告是遵从上帝的意愿。他不知道，其他官员都在暗中监视他，时刻准备着去大利乌王面前

指控他有罪。

禁令实施之后，官员们立刻向大利乌王指控但以理违反禁令。整整一天，大利乌王都不同意抓捕但以理，因为他非常欣赏这个男人，也知道他并没有错。但是，发布的禁令无法更改，他最后没有办法，只好妥协。

人们抓住了但以理，把他扔进狮子坑里，等着狮子把他撕成碎片。为了防止但以理逃脱，他们用沉重的石头把坑口堵住，还在上面加封了国王的印玺。

大利乌王担心他最忠诚的仆人的命运，因此不吃不喝，整夜不眠。天终于亮了，他急忙穿好衣服，冲到狮子坑那里，希望能发生奇迹，希望但以理还活着。

"但以理，你能听到吗？快告诉我，你的上帝是不是已经救你脱离狮子之口了！"

"啊，我的国王，"但以理回答，"正如你所说，上帝派天使封上了狮子之口。他不想让我死去，因为他看到了我的心，没有发现任何罪过，不论在上帝面前还是在国王面前，我都是无辜的。"

大利乌王喜极而泣，赶紧命人把但以理从狮子坑里拉出来，那些陷害但以理的卑鄙小人则被扔进了狮子坑。从此以后，但以理一直受到大利乌王和波斯人的敬重，正是他的正直救他脱离了狮子之口。

图书在版编目（CIP）数据

人类的故事／（意）曼纽拉·阿德雷亚尼绘；（意）费德丽卡·玛格林编；李静滢译. — 广州：广东人民出版社，2023.3

（镜子书·新编经典童话绘本系列）

ISBN 978-7-218-16031-3

Ⅰ.①人…　Ⅱ.①曼…　②费…　③李…　Ⅲ.①儿童故事—图画故事—意大利—现代　Ⅳ.① I546.85

中国版本图书馆CIP数据核字（2022）第175743号

RENLEI DE GUSHI

人 类 的 故 事

［意］曼纽拉·阿德雷亚尼　绘　　　［意］费德丽卡·玛格林　编　　　李静滢　译　　　　版权所有　翻印必究

出 版 人：肖风华

责任编辑：寇　毅
责任技编：吴彦斌　周星奎

出版发行：广东人民出版社
地　　址：广州市越秀区大沙头四马路 10 号（邮政编码：510199）
电　　话：（020）85716809（总编室）
传　　真：（020）83289585
网　　址：http://www.gdpph.com
印　　刷：北京尚唐印刷包装有限公司
开　　本：1000 毫米 ×1250 毫米　1/16
印　　张：4　　　　字　　数：36 千
版　　次：2023 年 3 月第 1 版
印　　次：2023 年 3 月第 1 次印刷
定　　价：78.00 元

如发现印装质量问题，影响阅读，请与出版社（020-87712513）联系调换。

售书热线：（020）87717307

饌
广®

出 品 人：许 永
出版统筹：林园林
责任编辑：寇 毅
特邀编辑：陈璐璟
装帧设计：李嘉木
印制总监：蒋 波
发行总监：田峰峥

发　　行：北京创美汇品图书有限公司
发行热线：010-59799930
投稿信箱：cmsdbj@163.com

官方微博

微信公众号

THE
STORIES
OF MANKIND

TEXT EDITED BY

FEDERICA MAGRIN

ILLUSTRATIONS BY

MANUELA ADREANI

CONTENTS

INTRODUCTION   3

CREATION   4

ADAM AND EVE   9

NOAH'S ARK   14

THE TOWER OF BABEL   19

JOSEPH AND HIS BROTHERS   22

SAMSON   29

DAVID AND GOLIATH   33

SOLOMON   36

JONAH   41

DANIEL IN THE LION'S DEN   44

INTRODUCTION

The Bible is the most widely read book in the world; indeed, for very many people, it is also the most important because it contains the teachings and the word of God, transcribed and collected by a variety of authors, at different times, in multiple languages, and assembled into many different books.

Did you know the word "bible" means "books" in ancient Greek? There are seventy-three books in the Bible, forty-six of which form the Old Testament and recount events between the creation of the world and the birth of Jesus. They describe the Hebrew people, their ancestors, their kings and the prophets who shaped history. Some very remarkable individuals come to life in these ancient texts!

The pages you are about to read present the most famous events described in the Bible. You'll meet Adam and Eve, Noah, Abraham, Moses, Joseph and other protagonists of the Old Testament.

You'll find their stories are full of lessons and advice, not to mention incredible adventures, promises broken and kept, mistakes, repentance and forgiveness, and essentially, faith and love.

CREATION

*B*efore the sky and land existed, chaos reigned on Earth. The world was a bleak, inhospitable place in which life was not possible. There were none of the great and extraordinary things we have around us today, like mountains, seas, plains and forests, and there was not a single, tiny creature in this dark and desolate land.

Prompted by a rush of boundless love, God began to create everything in the universe. He wanted the world to be perfect and it took him seven days to complete his work. This first thing he did was divide the water into two separate places, the water under and the water over, a primordial ocean of sorts, but with neither fish nor alga in it. It was a dark place in which chaos still reigned and no form of life, even the most basic, could survive.

It was for this reason that God decided there should be light – warm, powerful rays that would allow the future inhabitants of the world to thrive and multiply, without fear of the impenetrable darkness. The dark hours remained only at night, a time assigned to rest, in memory of the shadows and fear of old, and antithesis to the new light and hope.

After the first day, God divided the sky from the land, and named the canopy he created the firmament. He placed it up high so that it could be admired and make people dream when looking up at if *from far below.*

As the second day came to an end, God continued in his work, gathering together the water to form oceans, seas, lakes, rivers, streams and swamps. On the dry ground, which was occasionally wetted by water which fell as rain, he grew every kind of plant, creating enormous plains and forests to provide wood and shade. Some species of vegetation were made to bear fruit and seeds, so that they might multiply and grow dense.

The world was a much more welcoming place than before – the ideal environment for more complex life forms to develop.

On the fourth day, God added two great "lamps" to the things he had created so far: one big, bright one, the Sun, to provide light and warmth during the day; and another smaller, fainter one, the Moon, to brighten the nocturnal hours.

Creation was now ready to host living creatures.

And so on the fifth day, God commanded the seas, oceans, rivers and lakes to be filled with fish and other animals able to live underwater, like jellyfish, dolphins, whales; he bid the sky be populated with birds, small ones like hummingbirds, and also giant ones like pelicans, and all other winged animals that were able to fly.

Earth became an incredibly populated place. Creatures of unimaginable shapes and startling

colors swam in its waters, with fins to move quickly and gills to

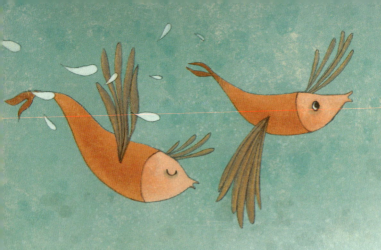

breath, while the blue sky was

invaded by chirping flocks of every kind of bird, some who beat their wings to move from place to place, others who soared on the wind. God was enchanted by his work and asked the sea creatures and the winged creatures to multiply and populate all corners of the planet, even the most remote that seemed impossible to reach.

His creation was truly wonderful and worthy of admiration, but God was still not satisfied. He

felt something important was missing and so, on the sixth day, he ordered the ground to be occupied by a profusion of animal species – cattle, like goats, oxen and sheep, which were easy to tame; wild beasts, like lions, elephants and bears, which were wild and difficult to approach; and reptiles, from tiny lizards to great snakes, destined *to forever crawl on the ground, eating dust lifted by their bodies.*

Everything he had created so far was great and deserving of praise, but God still felt something was missing, so did his best to make sure the world would be perfect by the time he finished. He ordered a living creature to be brought forth in his image, and in his own image he created people; he created them male and female, different but equally important, so that when they came together, they could have children and populate the earth.

To man and woman, God gave another important job, that of looking after the animals and

plants, tending them with love. From the land, they would have everything they needed to survive and proliferate, together with their children and their children's children, for many generations; they had herbs and seeds to feed on, others to feed to the cattle. They had everything they needed to eat and clothe themselves.

At the end of the sixth day, God looked at all that he had made and was supremely happy: above him was the firmament, with the Sun, the Moon and the stars to illuminate and show the way; below was the land, covered by water, forests, plains and deserts, where animals and mankind could live in peace. What he saw was the perfect reflection of his plan and a tangible sign of his immense love for the whole of creation.

On the seventh day, having completed his work, God decided to rest, to allow himself time to admire what he had created, in both the Sky and on Land. He did nothing the whole day but observe the incredible sight before his eyes, the marvel of the trees, the flowers, the animals and mankind, and from that moment, he decided the seventh day would be forever devoted to rest and reflection on how beautiful and unique Earth was.

This was how everything around us was created – the Universe, Earth and Living Creatures.

ADAM AND EVE

*The story of the first people dates to time immemorial, when the
Earth itself had just been*

*created. It was back then that God decided to take a handful of dust
from the ground and make it into the shape of a man – a mere pup-
pet that started to breathe and to move only when God breathed the
breath of life into his nostrils. For a home, God gave man the Garden of Eden, a place located eastward in which every kind of plant
grew and assured the new visitor a bounteous supply of fruit. In the
middle of the garden was a special tree, the tree of life, which gave
knowledge of good and evil. When God showed the man the many
wonders of the garden, he stated clearly that it was forbidden to eat
the fruit of this tree.*

*And so the man began his life in this enchanted place, eating the
plants and fruit that grew there and living a life without toil or labor.
Very soon, the man began to feel lonely, so God decided to surround
him with animals of all kinds.*

*One by one, he brought before the man the many creatures populat-
ing the skies, the land and the water, and asked him to give them a
name. The man named them all but despite being surrounded by a
multitude of different species, he still felt he hadn't found the com-
panion he sought.*

God realized that what the man needed was someone similar with whom to speak and share his day. He caused a deep sleep to fall on the man so that he could remove one of his ribs and, with it, create woman.

On reawakening, the man wondered at the beauty of the new creature moulded from his own

body and therefore a part of him. God ordered that they be considered husband and wife from that moment and that their union last in eternity. For some time, the couple lived happily in the garden, where they walked naked without feeling shame and had no worries of any kind.

The woman encountered a serpent one day and it asked her, "I heard you humans cannot eat the fruit of the tree of life. Is this true?"

The woman replied, "We can take any fruit we wish, but not from the tree in the center of the garden. If we do, we will die right away."

The serpent replied that this was not true, and they would never risk death by eating only one

piece of fruit. "If anything," he continued, persuasively, "you will be like God and know everything if you do."

The woman went to look closer and noticed for the first time that the fruit on the tree of life was more enticing than all the others. She thought for a long time about what the serpent had said and was unable to resist. She picked a fruit and took it to her husband.

*They ate it together whereupon they became aware of their naked-
ness. The fruit had given them knowledge of good and evil they had
not had before, and it made them sew fig leaves together to cover
themselves.*

*Moments later, on hearing God approach, the man ran to hide behind
a plant.*

"Why did you run away?" God asked when he saw the man hiding.

"Because I am ashamed that I am naked."

*Surprised at the man's reply, God asked, "How do you know you
are naked?" then continued, "Have you eaten from the tree of life?"
The man nodded, and God asked why he had done it.*

*"My wife brought the fruit to me and I succumbed to the temptation
to taste it."*

*God turned to the woman, "Why did you do this when I told you it
was forbidden?"*

*The woman told of how she had met the serpent and it had deceived
her, telling her that nothing serious would happen if she ate from the
tree of life.*

*God became angry and cursed the serpent. "For what you have done,
you and all your descendants shall be condemned to crawl on the
ground and eat dust.*

*Between you and the woman there shall be no friendship, only ha-
tred.*

 11

You will try to bite her heel and she will crush you with her foot."

God's anger then turned on the man and woman, to whom he announced they would now have to toil to obtain from the ground the things they had previously picked without effort. After imposing their punishment, God ordered both man and woman to leave the wonders of Eden and to live forever in hostile lands.

When they were forced to abandon their earthly paradise, the man took the name Adam and he named his wife Eve, because she would be the mother of all men.

From their union, two very different children were born, Cain and Abel. Growing up, Cain wanted to be a farmer and Abel a shepherd. When the boys had become men, they decided to offer up to God part of their daily produce one day. Cain gathered the most succulent fruit while Abel sacrificed a few of his sheep. God favored Abel's sacrifice more, and Cain lost his temper with both the Lord and his brother. His anger mounted until he could endure it no longer and one merciless day, he murdered Abel.

When God learned what Cain had done, he drove him from the land and banished him to a life without peace, wandering from place to place. He would also have to work much harder than before to reap even the smallest of fruits from the land.

Cain accepted his fate and settled in Nod, opposite Eden. He met a woman, they married, and she gave birth to a child, Enoch, who built

a city and became the head of a large family.

Adam and Eve also had another child, named Set. He brought new joy to the couple after they lost their first two children, one murdered, the other sent away.

NOAH'S ARK

For a long time, the world was an enchanted place in which animals and man lived together in peace. Bubbles burst forth from the silver waters of rivers while brightly-colored fish leapt through them; the cold depths of lakes provided a home to creatures of every type; and the powerful waves of the sea hid animals of the most wonderful shapes and sizes. The forests were leafy and dense, the mountains lined with shrubs and vegetation, the mountaintops coated with snow all year around, while the verdant plains were crossed by herds of grazing animals, predators following on their heels. Birds circled the skies while the animals had learned to live together in the deserts, forests and prairies. There was food enough for everyone and harmony reigned supreme.

But this joyful time was soon replaced by a much sadder one.

Men and women had become greedy and arrogant, they had forgotten the beauty of the natural world around them and how they should thank God for it all. War, corruption and enmity had replaced peace, justice and kindness. Even animals could no longer find a peaceful way of living together. The whole of creation was once again in the grip of chaos.

God waited and watched, hoping humanity would repent and return to obeying his laws, but the day came when he realized nothing

could restore his kingdom to its former glory. Bitterly disappointed, he decided he would have to start afresh, like an artist rejecting a painting and reaching out for a blank new canvas. The only way to achieve it was a flood that would sweep away all that was wicked and allow the few remaining good things to flourish once more.

For this task, God chose Noah. Unlike other men, Noah had continued to behave as God required, looking after his family, tending to the animals in his care, and honoring God every day.

"Noah," God said, "it is with a heavy heart that I have decided to send a great storm that will flood the world and wipe out wickedness forthwith. I don't want anything to happen to you or your family, quite the opposite, I want you to be able to start a new humanity that is kinder and more just. For this reason, I ask you to build an ark, an enormous vessel that is big enough to hold seven pairs of clean animals and two pairs of unclean animals. Use strong wood and daub it inside and out with pitch to make it watertight. You must also build a roof on top to stop the rain from entering. I will warn you when the time comes, so you can bring inside the animals, your family and enough food for all."

Noah was shocked at what he heard but did exactly as God commanded, sawing planks of sturdy wood and joining them together to build the ark. When the great vessel was complete, he daubed it with tar and filled it with food.

God returned to Noah and announced that the floods would soon come. "In seven days, I will make the rains start and they will last forty days and forty nights. Prepare everything before that day comes, as I have advised, and you will be safe."

Noah, who was six hundred years old at the time, again did as he was instructed. He herded the many species of animals inside the ark then asked his wife, their three children, Sem, Cam and Iafet, and their wives, to take refuge onboard.

The seventh day came, the sky filled with dark clouds, and outside it became as black as night.

The Sun disappeared, and in its place, a blanket of darkness fell over Earth. Seconds later, torrential rain began to crash down, cold and fierce, beating on the trees and houses. Water engulfed the plains and forests, and the oceans grew so big and violent they broke their banks and flooded the deserts and hills. As time went on, Earth vanished from sight. Even the highest mountaintop disappeared under a *sheet of black, angry water.*

The Ark floated on the surface, at the mercy of the heaving waters, and looking out of the tiny window at the top, Noah couldn't see anything bar the storm that raged on.

It remained thus for forty days and forty nights. Inside the Ark, Noah, his family and all their animals were safe, they ate the food they had packed and waited for the storm to end with hope in their hearts.

A howling wind whipped up from nowhere, the gusts so violent they swept away the clouds and dried up some of the water. In the seventh month after the flood, the ark carrying Noah and the animals came to rest atop Mount Ararat, and after another three months, mountaintops began to reappear around them.

The world still seemed under water, so Noah sent out a raven then a dove to find somewhere to build a new home. Both returned, having found no trace of dry land.

The flood had been so mighty, they had to wait several more days before the water receded enough. When Noah finally sent the dove out again in search of a sign, it returned with an olive branch in its beak. Noah could hardly contain his joy – Earth was flourishing once again, and producing trees and flowers. God had kept his promise and they were safe!

"Noah," God called him, "you and your family can now leave the

ark. The world has returned to what it once was, and it will be home to you and all the animals you have brought with you, now and for generations in the future. You have my blessing and I promise to never again send such a mighty flood. As a sign of this covenant, a bow of many colors will form in the sky to remember the bond between the sky and the land." As God spoke, an enormous rainbow appeared in the sky.

"All those who see it will remember this promise and God's love for all creatures who laud him with a good and righteous life."

Noah became a farmer. He would occasionally raise his eyes to the sky as he happily tended his vines, seeking out the rainbow that would remind him of God's promise - to him, his children and to the new world he'd created.

*P*eople were not always divided into nations, their lands were not always divided by borders, and men could once speak easily to one another, having just one language that they all understood. As a result, people who lived in the north were equal to those who lived in the south, and those who had decided to settle in the east resembled those who had set up home in the west. People lived together in peace and came together regularly to celebrate the extraordinary world that God had given them.

There came a day, however, when some men settled in a land called Shinar, in the far east, and built a city that was bigger and more spectacular than any other. They wanted to rival nature and create something that would equal the magnificence of the mountains, forests and oceans.

Such a construction had never been attempted before, and to build this one, the people baked an endless supply of bricks in enormous kilns. Bricks would be much stronger than the stone normally used, and by bonding the bricks with tar, they would withstand the weather much better than simple mortar.

They agreed to erect an enormous tower in the center of the city, one so high it would reach the sky, and so grand anyone seeing it would gaze in amazement. Anyone looking up at it from below would not be able to see the top, which would reach into the clouds.

The construction of the houses and public buildings in the city required considerable effort. Craftsmen and laborers, led by architects and engineers, worked day and night, year after year, to complete the many buildings, but erecting the tower was an even more gruelling task.

The people looked on with pride as the building of the tower progressed, floor after floor.

"It's the most beautiful thing ever created!" someone exclaimed.

"Nothing in nature can compare to the tower!" someone else applauded.

"Now that we have the tower, we need a name that sets us apart from the rest of the world," someone suggested.

"Yes," someone else replied. "We're not like anyone else. We have built this city and this magnificent tower!"

"Right," yet someone else echoed. *"We are different. We are better because we have built something unique and unsurpassable."*

Their clamor reached the ears of God, who was always listening and watching over Creation. He was deeply wounded at what he heard as he had created mankind to live in harmony with each other, no one person superior or inferior to another, and sharing the world with animals. He had not created man from dust so that he might challenge God and try to take his place!

He was disappointed with the people who had erected the tower and those who had praised it, but God realized it was in man's nature to want to excel and rival God. He did not strike the tower down with a bolt of lightning nor did he send a messenger to bring humanity to its senses; what he did was cause the people, from that day, to divide into different lands and

to have different characteristics, immediately speaking a different way.

The city was abandoned and the grand tower it hosted become known as the Tower of Babel, meaning "confused and chaotic place."

Indeed, it was after its construction that people started to speak different languages, making communication between peoples almost impossible.

JOSEPH AND HIS BROTHERS

*J*acob had many children and although he loved them all like only a father can, he had a genuine preference for the youngest, because he had been born to him in his old age when he thought he would have no more children. From birth, Joseph had held a special place in his father's heart which was why Jacob directed most of his attentions to him and lavished precious gifts upon him.

The elder brothers were jealous, even more so when Joseph began to have premonitory dreams in which it became clear his life would be special and they would all have to bow before him.

Jacob asked Joseph one day to check if all was going well with his brothers, who had taken the sheep to graze near Shechem. To please his father, whom he loved dearly, the young Joseph set off to reach his brothers. When they saw him arrive, they plotted to kill him. Luckily, they changed their minds at the last minute and sold him to a trader headed to Egypt instead.

So, for twenty shekels of silver, Joseph was taken as a slave to the distant land of Egypt while his brothers returned home to tell their father that his beloved youngest son had been torn apart by a wild beast.

While Jacob wept in Canaan for his son's death, Joseph found himself serving in the household of Potiphar, a very powerful man and

captain of the Pharaoh's guard. Within no time, Joseph proved to his master that he could administer with skill the many things entrusted to him. As a result, Potiphar gave Joseph charge of the palace. Unfortunately, Potiphar's wife also laid eyes on Joseph and became enamored of him. Feeling a duty of respect towards the man who had taken him under his wing, Joseph refused the woman. He could never have imagined she would seek revenge and cause him to be arrested and imprisoned.

Joseph was not only his father's favourite, he was also very much loved by God, who has been secretly watching over him since his birth. It was with God's divine intervention that the prison warden recognized Joseph's talents and gave him an important role in the running of the prison.

During his imprisonment, Joseph was often summoned to interpret dreams. It was a gift he had always possessed, and which set him apart from everyone else.

This same skill brought him not long after before the Pharaoh. The Egyptian king had had two nightmares which worried him a great deal. In fact, he felt they had been sent to warn him about something, but he couldn't make any sense of them.

The royal cupbearer advised the Pharaoh to summon Joseph who had once helped him interpret a dream. Joseph was called before the king.

"I can find no peace," the Pharaoh said. "A few nights ago, I dreamt of seven fat cows and then seven lean cows, and then seven good ears of corn which dried up before my eyes. I know it must mean something, but I don't know what..."

"The seven fat cows, like the seven good ears of corn, are seven years of plenty," Joseph explained, "whereas the seven lean cows and seven dry ears of corn are seven years of hunger. You must gather enough wheat in the years of plenty so that you will not suffer when the ground becomes arid and produces no fruit in the years of hunger."

The Pharaoh was deeply troubled by what Joseph said. If what the man had foretold was correct, he would have to be extremely careful or his kingdom could end up without food in the drought years. Despite his initial puzzlement, the king believed Joseph's interpretation and decided to appoint him administrator of the kingdom, giving him his ring to signal they would be equals in governing decisions.

And so the former slave and prisoner was given the task of managing the country's resources and assure its prosperity. As foretold, for seven years abundant rain fell, rendering the fields fertile and producing wheat that exceeded their expectations. Now viceroy, Joseph ordered all surpluses to be kept in the storehouses. After seven years of abundance, when water no longer fell on the desert plains and the plants began to wither, the storehouses were opened to feed the people and animals.

Now, you should know that the drought affected not only the area around the river Nile, but also vast neighboring areas, including Canaan. Jacob sent his sons to Egypt with enough money to buy grain for their family and their animals.

After many years, the brothers found themselves face-to-face with Joseph.

As you can imagine, they didn't recognize him and believing him to be a man of importance, bowed before him. Joseph had no trouble remembering his brothers or what they had done to him. For this reason, he wished to accuse them of being spies and have the guards throw them out. But he thought twice about it and decided to seek an agreement with them instead. He would give them wheat if they returned with their younger brother, the son born to Jacob and Joseph's mother after Joseph had gone away to Egypt. News that he had a younger brother had moved him deeply and he desperately wanted to meet him!

Joseph's brothers, laden with wheat given to them by a man they believed the viceroy of Egypt, returned to their father and told him of the governor's request.

For a long time, Jacob refused to send his youngest son Benjamin to a distant, foreign land. He feared he might lose him as had happened with his beloved Joseph.

The time came, though, when their food stores began to run so low he had to relent.

The brothers, Benjamin included, set off on foot for Egypt to meet the viceroy again.

Joseph welcomed them enthusiastically. Even though his brothers had been very cruel to him, he couldn't help but love them dearly.

Unaware they were before their brother, Jacob's sons were astonished at the vehicle sent to invite them to dinner with the governor and his family. When the viceroy later gave them the wheat they had asked for and granted them leave, they were surprised and scared, as if plagued by a sense of foreboding.

On the way home, they were stopped by some Egyptian soldiers who checked their sacks. A silver cup was found in Benjamin's. Joseph had instructed his men to hide it there to put his brothers to a final test. On their return to the palace, Joseph revealed his true identity and tested their love for Benjamin, saying that he would keep the boy who had stolen the cup. The brothers stepped forward and begged Joseph not to do it. They were scared of having to return a second time to their father with news that he'd lost another son. Moved by the gesture, Joseph invited them to go back to Canaan and bring their father and the rest of the family to Egypt.

Jacob was initially reluctant to leave the land of his forefathers but decided, in the end, to tackle the journey.

On arriving in Egypt, he would be able to embrace the son he had long thought dead.

When he died many years later, the joy of spending the last years of his life surrounded by all his sons, was imprinted on his face.

The brothers feared that, on the death of their father, the viceroy would finally take his revenge. They did not know that Joseph had not pretended to forgive them to please their father, it had been sincere and from the bottom of his heart.

"Do not be afraid," he reassured them when they were gathered together in the palace. "I do not want to harm you. If God intended things to go in a certain way, it was to bring us to what we are today – a family and a people reunited in one place, with no concern for famine or worse danger."

Joseph was magnanimous to those who had treated him unfairly and was rewarded with a long and happy life. He saw his children grow and his grandchildren come into the world, before he closed his eyes for the last time in the tranquillity of his own home, at the age of one hundred and ten.

SAMSON

*A*ll children are special, although some more than others. God chooses them for the great feats they perform and causes their birth to be seen as a miracle.

THIS IS WHAT HAPPENED TO SAMSON, WHO WAS BORN TO BECOME A HERO, A SAVIOR OF HIS PEOPLE.

In these times, the Israelites were subjugated to the Philistines, who treated them with scorn and prevented them from living as they would have liked. Many people hoped someone might come along and help them regain their freedom.

In one of the cities administered by the Philistines there lived Manoah, a kind and reverent Israelite, married to an equally good and religious woman. Unfortunately, and to their great sorrow, the couple were childless. An angel visited the woman one day and announced she would soon be a mother. The woman was surprised, even more so when she learned that the child, to be consecrated to God from conception, would live his life by some very specific rules. He would never eat impure foods, for example, or cut his hair.

Fearing she may not have fully understood the words of the divine messenger, the woman called her husband, to whom the angel repeated the precepts by which they would be required to abide.

It was under such auspices that Samson was born. As he grew, his strength and courage were so great he became famous, and the young boy was feared and respected wherever he went. But in tandem with these qualities, Samson had a predisposition that caused him not to see the dangers that lay on his path and to get into trouble. Indeed, in Timnah he fell hopelessly in love with a young Philistine girl and determined to marry her, despite the disapproval of his parents who feared serious disaccord between their son and his wife's family.

Their fears were justified. Incomprehension between Samson and the Philistines led to armed conflict, after which the young man was taken prisoner by the people of Judah, who feared reprisals by the Philistines. As Samson was being led to the latter, he managed to free himself. The tight bindings were unable to contain the might of his muscles, and they snapped, crumpling to his feet like charred flax.

Free to fight

back once again, he grabbed the closest thing to hand, the jawbone of a dead donkey and swung it like an iron mace, quickly striking down an army of one thousand men.

On conclusion of this great feat, Samson called to God for some water and, miraculously, a fountain gurgled forth at his feet.

Following these events, Samson moved to Gaza, and thus to the Valley of Sorek, where he met a beautiful woman with whom he became infatuated. Her name was Delilah but her beauty hid a secret – she had been instructed by Philistine princes to find out everything she could about their enemy.

And so it was that with great artifice and cunning Delilah tried to discover Samson's secret. If she could find out, the Philistines would be able to defeat him once and for all.

For a long time, Samson lied to Delilah, telling her he could be beaten if he were to be bound with seven fresh bowstrings, or with new ropes, or if the braids on his head were secured to a door. Each time the woman told the Philistines, who tried, unsuccessfully, to do what had been suggested.

A day came, however, when Samson was no longer able to deceive Delilah – he loved her too much to continue in his deceit.

"You must know," he said, "that my strength lies in my hair, which has never been cut. If someone were to cut it, I would be as weak as any other man."

When night came, Delilah put Samson to sleep on her lap and cut his hair.

The Philistines, who had been waiting outside, burst into the room, blinded Samson and took him to Gaza where he was put in shackles and made to turn the grindstone.

Humiliated and scorned, Samson spent his days in the depths of despair, while all the time his hair began to grow again.

The Philistine rulers decided to offer a sacrifice to their god Dagon. Hundreds of people had gathered in the great ceremonial room and Samson was led in to entertain them as court jester.

Samson used the opportunity to execute God's plan. Resting against the pillars on which the temple stood, he cried, "Lord, I beg you, restore the strength I was given at birth. Let me die with the Philistines!" Then he broke the pillars holding up the temple and brought the building down on them. And so Samson met his fate, a hero who had lost his way on account of a deceitful love, but ultimately recovered his lost vigor and courage to let fate take its course.

DAVID AND GOLIATH

*I*magine a young child, a little bigger than you, taking on a giant. Sounds incredible, doesn't it? Yet, it's what David, the boy who became king of Israel, did. But first things first...

At the time of this story, Israel's army was camped at Ephes Dammim, ready to go to battle against the army of the Philistines, gathered nearby and poised for the imminent clash.

The Philistine's champion, a certain Goliath from Gath, a seemingly invincible man of immense proportions and winner of countless battles, would emerge from his tent every day - clad in heavy armor that gleamed in the sun and brandishing weapons like mere twigs in his hands - and dare soldiers of the enemy army to face him in a duel. The Israelites were scared by the mere roar of Goliath's booming voice and refused to fight a warrior of his stature. This had led to a stalemate and no one knew how to resolve it.

David, a young, red-haired boy who normally helped with his father's flocks, came to the camp one day. He'd only come to check how his brothers were getting on and take their pay back to his father, but he was fascinated by Goliath and became curious about the nature of the problem.

Saul, the king of Israel, learned of the boy's presence and his curiosity, and summoned him to demand an explanation.

Without waiting for the king to address him, David said, "I will fight for you!" Surprised, Saul replied, "But you are just a boy, what makes you think you can take on a strong and able warrior?"

David reassured him, "I have faced beasts of all kinds, like lions and bears, taking my father's sheep to pasture, and I have always overcome them because I have God on my side."

Saul tried to convince the boy to at least don some armor, but David preferred to brave the enemy with only his trusted sling and five stones gathered from a brook.

When Goliath saw him approach, he burst out laughing then, serious once again, threatened to smash him to pieces and feed his body to the animals.

David replied that, with God's help, he would beat the giant, whose death would bring about the fall of the entire Philistine army. David advanced fearlessly toward the great warrior, withdrew a stone from his pouch, placed it in the sling, and fired it at his opponent's forehead. Goliath fell to the ground. David went straight over to the giant and cut off his head with his own sword.

The Philistines fled the instant they saw what had happened, the Israelite soldiers close behind them.

David was hailed in triumph and praised for his deeds. A young boy had beaten a warrior with guile and, most importantly, through his faith in God. All he had needed was a sling and immense courage

to get the better of a warrior who believed in nothing other than his own strength.

SOLOMON

*H*eroes are usually characterized by their bravery and strength, on rare occasions they are also endowed with great wisdom, a gift that God grants to very few. Solomon was one of the fortunate champions of antiquity who was given the chance to be wiser than any other man on Earth. It was Solomon himself, responding to God one day, who asked for such a gift. As king, he could have asked for riches, eternal life, beauty, strength, everything a powerful man might desire, but instead, he had begged the Lord to be forever guided by reason, that he might be a good leader of the kingdom left to him by his father David.

His great wisdom became the topic of much rumor and people travelled from far and wide to his palace to put his good judgment to the test. Two women came to stand before him one day, both claiming to be the real mother of the same child. "This woman and I," the first woman began, "lived in the same house when we both gave birth to a baby. I fell asleep with my baby beside me one night, but when I awoke the morning after, my baby was dead. When I looked more closely, I saw the

37

dead baby wasn't the son I had borne but the other woman's, who had stolen mine when her own baby died."

"That's not true!" the other woman protested when it was her turn to speak. "The child in my arms is the one I bore and kept with me from that moment. This woman lost her baby and wants to replace him with mine, but I will never allow it!"

Having heard both versions, Solomon thought for a while then left the room. He returned seconds later holding a long, sharp sword in his hand.

"Since we cannot know who the child really belongs to and you both want him, I will now cut the child in half so you can each have a part," Solomon ruled imperiously, leaving the people in the room speechless.

"No, don't do it!" one of the two women screamed, agonized. "I'd rather my son lived with her than die."

"Do it!" the other woman cried in response, "Then we will both be happy."

Solomon smiled, now he knew which of the two women was the true mother of the child.

"Only a mother would do anything for her child, renouncing the chance to raise him to keep him from harm. The woman willing to kill the child is lying and does not deserve any pity. Give the baby to the first woman."

38

This was only one of Solomon's many judgments and fame of his wisdom spread far and wide, even travelling beyond his kingdom and into distant lands.

News had also reached the Queen of Sheba, who was so fascinated by the idea of the wise Solomon that she decided to make the long journey to test his knowledge. On reaching the king's court, she began to question him, devising a series of intricate stratagems to try to catch him out and prove he was a man like any other. In the end, she had to admit that Solomon possessed something divine, something out of the ordinary, and she complimented him on his wit and intelligence.

When the Queen was led through the rooms of the palace to witness their splendor, she was doubly surprised – despite being accustomed to ostentation and wealth, she could never have imagined a human mind able of conceiving something so grand and perfect as that wonderful palace.

Before taking her leave of Solomon, she decided to give him a tangible sign of her appreciation. She brought him one hundred and twenty gifts of gold and large quantities of aromatic spices and priceless stones.

Solomon accepted the gifts out of respect for his guest, but it was the queen's words he most appreciated – "Blessed be your kingdom, the people who surround you, the country that benefits from your

leadership and God, who gave you such wisdom."

Indeed, being wiser than any man, Solomon knew that "a good name is worth more than great wealth, respect more than gold and silver."

JONAH

*E*vents involving the prophet Jonah were extraordinary and mirac-
ulous, the most incredible to ever happen to a man – a turbulent trip
at sea, a close encounter with a creature of monstrous proportions
and preaching in a foreign land.

Why did they all happen? Because God wanted to test Jonah who, in
his heart of hearts, doubted the message he had received.

The Lord appeared to Jonah one day and asked him to go to the
city of Nineveh to convert the people who had become wicked and
dishonest.

But Jonah was afraid, believing the task too difficult to complete.
Instead, he went in the opposite direction and boarded a ship bound
for Tarshish.

The ship had just left port when a terrible storm broke. The waves
were big enough to capsize the craft and winds so powerful they

ripped the sails, stopping them from sailing in the right direction.

The sailors were frightened and wondered what would happen to them, now that they were at the mercy of the waves and the storm which raged around them. Jonah, who knew only too well that the storm had been sent by God because he had not kept his promise, took pity on the terrified men and told them that, to placate God's fury, they should throw him into the sea and leave him to his fate.

Reluctantly, the crew did as they were instructed, and Jonah found himself in the water, which had all of a sudden become flat.

There were more trials in store for Jonah. God sent a large fish to devour him. For three days and three nights, Jonah was held captive in the monster's stomach but after humbly begging the Lord's forgiveness, was freed on the seashore.

"Will you now go to Nineveh as I asked?" God asked Jonah again.

Without answering, Jonah set off for the city of sin, wishing to please the Lord. On his arrival, he began to preach the word of the Lord and very quickly rid the people of the wickedness that had taken over their souls.

Instead of rejoicing at his success, Jonah was furious. Deep down, he'd wanted the people of Nineveh to be indifferent to his message and for God to raze the city to the ground.

To prove to Jonah he was mistaken, God caused a leafy castor oil plant to grow over the hut Jonah had built just outside the city walls.

The prophet was very happy because the plant provided shade he could sleep more easily under. But the next day, a worm chewed the plant's roots and the plant withered.

Lying in his house, hot in the scorching rays of the sun, Jonah wished to die.

But God said, "You are angry with a castor oil plant you did not tend and which grew and withered in only a short time, yet I should not be concerned with the fate of an entire city that is home to thousands of people?"

Jonah understood. The Lord's mercy was too big for a prophet to comprehend. Nineveh may have done wrong, but the repentance the people had shown fully justified their salvation.

DANIEL IN THE LION'S DEN

*D*uring the reign of King Darius the Mede in Persia, there lived a righteous and reverent man, a loyal servant of his king and strict observer of the Law of God. His name was Daniel and it was to Daniel that the king assigned an important role in government, making him his equal in the most important decisions. This appointment caused a stir in the royal palace, arousing intense jealousy in the hearts of the other officials assigned more minor responsibilities. They schemed together to find something of which to accuse poor Daniel, who was oblivious to what was being plotted behind his back.

Unable to find anything in his behavior that could cast Daniel in a poor light, the officials decided to set a trap. They requested a private audience with the king and asked him to reconfirm an ancient law whereby anyone praying for more than thirty days to a god or a man that was not the king would be put to death. On seeing Darius' perplexity over whether to sign the decree, they pointed out that it was essential to restore the glorious past of the Medes and Persians. The king finally accepted to sign the injunction, not realizing his commissioners intended it as a way of condemning Daniel who, in line with his precepts, opened his window towards Jerusalem and the Holy Land three times a day to pray to the Lord God.

Daniel knew about the law but decided not to stop praying because *he was sure he was doing nothing wrong; if anything, he was doing what the Lord God wished of him. He wasn't to know the commissioners were secretly spying on him in order to refer his guilt back to the king.*

After the prescribed time, the commissioners rushed straight to Darius to accuse Daniel. For a whole day, the king refused to order Daniel's capture, he was fond of the man and knew he had done nothing wrong. However, forced by a law that allowed no revocation, he had to capitulate.

Daniel was arrested and left in the lion's den to be torn apart by the beasts. A heavy stone was set over the pit to stop him from escaping, and the king made if official by placing his own seal on top.

Darius spent the night fasting, lying awake and thinking about the fate of his most loyal servant. When the sun rose, he dressed and rushed to the lion's pit in the hope a miracle might have occurred and Daniel was still alive.

"Daniel, please, talk to me! Tell me that your God has saved you from the lions!" he shouted.

"Oh my King," Daniel replied from the pit, "It happened just as you described. My God sent an angel to shut the lions' mouths. He didn't want me to die because he looked into my heart and found no sin, not against him or against you."

Darius cried tears of joy and ordered Daniel to be pulled from the

lion's den. The commissioners who had behaved so despicably, condemning an innocent man, were to be put there in his place.

For the rest of his days, Daniel was respected and esteemed by his king and the people of Persia – he was the man whose immense faith had saved him from the lions.